THE BLESSING
OF THE BEASTS

the Blessing of the Beasts

By Ethel Pochocki

Illustrated by Barry Moser

PARACLETE PRESS ❦ 2007
BREWSTER, MASSACHUSETTS

The Blessing of the Beasts

2007 First Printing

Text copyright © 2007 by Ethel Pochocki

Illustrations copyright © 2007 by Barry Moser

ISBN 978-1-55725-502-0

Calligraphy by Judythe Sieck

Library of Congress Cataloging-in-Publication Data
Pochocki, Ethel, 1925-
The blessing of the beasts / by Ethel Pochocki; illustrated by
Barry Moser. p. cm.
Summary: Martin the skunk and Francesca the cockroach wend their
way across the city to attend the blessing of the animals
celebration on the Feast of St. Francis.
ISBN 978-1-55725-502-0
[1. Cockroaches—Fiction. 2. Skunks—Fiction. 3. Animals—Fiction.
4. Benediction—Fiction.] I. Moser, Barry, ill. II. Title.
PZ7.P7495Bl 2007
[E]—dc22   2007002231

10 9 8 7 6 5 4 3 2 1

Published by Paraclete Press

Brewster, Massachusetts

www.paracletepress.com

Printed in Singapore

For the dogs—Emily, Rosie, Moose,
and cats—Nora, Dandy, Pansy, Mamacats 1 & 2,
Lefty, Beatrice, Josephine, Chester, Teddy, and Vinnie
who have blessed my life,
and Lucien, Gingerella, Gracie, Leo,
Annie, Colette, Poppy, Damien,
and Mouse
who bless it still
—EP

And for the beautiful beasts that bless my life:
Mina, Mehitabel, Murray, Little Mac, Roxanne,
and especially my big, sweet
IKE.
And in loving memory of Obie and Woody,
and especially the memories of
Truman and Rosie,
my blessed
and departed companions.
—BM

Three young uptown roaches.

WORD OF THE celebration arrived at St. Francis soup kitchen shortly after breakfast by way of three young uptown roaches. They arrived in a crate of discarded supermarket vegetables, hidden within the leaves of wilted lettuce.

They skittered across the floor, carefully avoiding the humans' sandaled feet, into the woodwork beneath the sink. Once secure behind the drainboard, they danced around their sleeping cousins, crying, "Wake up! We've got news!"

The cousins woke, grumpy and annoyed at being disturbed, for they had been up all night. Erasmus, the roach elder of the community, groped for his glasses and demanded in a stern voice to know what was going on.

The uptown roaches fell over themselves gibbering and giggling and interrupting each other. "Wait till you hear — there's to be a celebration in the cathedral for creatures!"

"Whatever for?" growled Erasmus, scratching his hairy legs.

"It's for Francis, the good human. They're having a giant party and everyone's invited. There'll be food and music and dancing and people whose pockets we can crawl into."

"You mean the soup kitchen's Francis?" asked a young female roach.

"The very one."

Erasmus, the roach elder of the community.

I was named for him, you know.

"Lovely! I was named for him, you know," she said proudly. And she told the story of how after she was born, in this very kitchen, her mother called her Francesca, in honor of the human who loved the unlovable. Now there was to be a party for him, and she was invited to it.

"Before you get all worked up," said Erasmus, yawning, "we won't be going. The trip's too dangerous. And even if we made it, do you think they'd let us in? They'd get their spray guns out in a flash and zap us. So you better get on home, boys. Thanks for the invite, but no thanks."

The young roaches left and the others went to sleep—all except Francesca, who wondered what it would be like inside a church. Her mother had told her there was no reason to visit such a place. Churches were disgustingly clean, barren of food, although sometimes you might find leftover wedding rice under the pews, and they were dangerous.

She knew personally of one entire roach family tragically wiped out as they nibbled on the hymnals, mercilessly crushed by the cleaning woman. "They went singing into Paradise, just like the martyrs," sighed her mother.

But this would be different, Francesca thought, as she headed for the alley outside. She would ask Martin about it. He was older and wiser and would know about churches. Martin, who was a skunk, and Francesca had been friends since they met in a trash can a while back. He had startled her by rising from the garbage, wearing a cap of coleslaw and a mustache of yogurt.

"Good evening, Miss," he said, remembering his manners. "My name is Martin. After the saint,

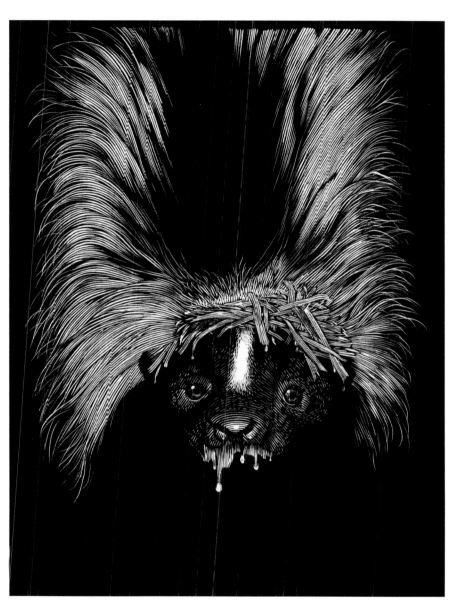

Good evening, Miss. My name is Martin.

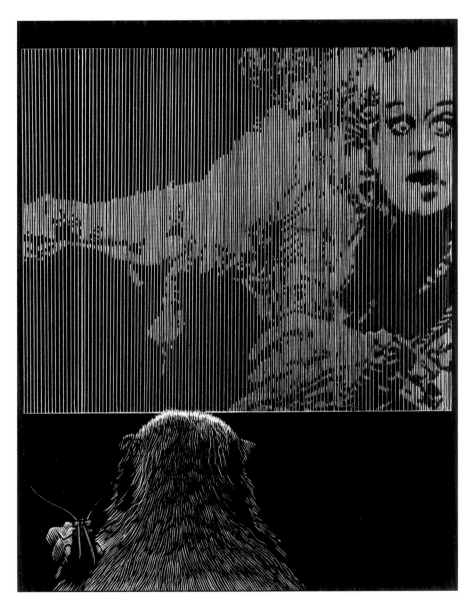

Sometimes they went to the movies and ate popcorn.

Martin de Porres. My mother favored him. His statue was in the garden where we ate, so she named me, her firstborn, after him. And your name is . . . ?"

"Francesca."

"How elegant. Your grandmother's name, perhaps?"

Francesca explained about her name and everything else she knew about herself. Martin did the same, and they discovered that they had much in common.

Every night after their first meeting, they met and shared meals and went exploring. Sometimes they went to the movies, where they sat in the balcony and ate popcorn. Sometimes they sat by the lake in the park, feeding Twinkies to the ducks. Sometimes they just sat and pondered life and its mysteries.

Tonight Francesca excitedly shared her news about the celebration with Martin. "And the priest will bless all the animals. Can you imagine? I've never been blessed before."

"Nor have I," replied Martin smiling, "but I don't think we are meant to be included, Francesca. It's for the respectables, the cute and cuddlies."

"Well," said Francesca, "I'll bet there'll be rats and snakes and porcupines there. We're as cute as they are."

"We are outcasts, my dear," said Martin gently. "They'll never let us in. Can't you just hear the humans shrieking as we walk down the aisle? They'd be fainting left and right."

"We don't have to go down the aisle," persisted Francesca, "we could watch from the back of the church."

We are outcasts, my dear.

Oh, Martin, there's more to life than garbage.

"And what would we see? Nothing but legs."

"We could still hear the music and smell the flowers and be part of the excitement. Oh, Martin, there's more to life than garbage."

"All right, we'll go." Martin shook his head wearily. How could he resist Francesca? "But we've got to plan this carefully, logically. Proceed with caution. Now, the ceremony begins at nine AM. We must start at four AM. It's some distance, you know, from the kitchen to the cathedral. Can you handle it?"

"Can you? All I do is ride along on your tail."

"Tail might be too dangerous. I think you should settle into my left ear. That way you won't be blown off."

"Won't I make your ear itch?"

"Can't feel a thing. A car hit me on that side and now the ear just takes up space. You might as well use it."

And so, as they finished off a crust of asparagus quiche, they planned their journey. Martin knew the shortcuts through parks and subways and playgrounds. By using them, they should arrive at the cathedral about 8:45 AM, if they didn't run into trouble.

On the morning of October 4, at exactly 4:36 AM (they overslept), Martin, with Francesca aboard, set off at a brisk waddle. "Rejoicing, we go on our way," laughed Francesca, snuggling into her furry berth.

They had several close calls within the hour. Once, as Martin crossed a street, Francesca leaned over too far and fell out. When Martin stopped to retrieve her, they were almost hit by a yellow cab. Then a boy threw an empty wine bottle at him. Fortunately, his aim was bad, but Martin had to make a long detour around the island of broken glass.

Fortunately his aim was bad.

Martin slipped into the van and hid among the flowers.

And he caused a near panic in the subway when he tried to squeeze through the door with a bunch of nurses. He escaped back onto the platform just before the door slammed shut.

"Phew," gasped Francesca, after they made their way back up to the street. "This uptown life isn't for me. How much longer?"

Martin sniffed the air. "No burnt coffee, French fries, fried fish, no grease at all. I'd say we're almost there."

At that moment, a van stopped in front of them. The driver got out, slid open the side door and went into a florist shop. "Hey," he yelled inside, "got those flowers for the animal bash?"

Quickly Martin slipped into the van and hid behind a bucket of giant chrysanthemums. The driver brought more buckets of asters and sunflowers that made the air smell brisk and fresh.

The door slid shut, and the van started up and lurched forward. "This is wonderful," Martin said with a smile, as Francesca leaned out to touch a sunflower petal. "This will take us right to the door."

When they arrived at the cathedral, Martin and Francesca hid themselves in a yew bush and watched as the animals with their humans began their parade through the huge bronze doors.

A great, deep voice from the altar sang out, "Let the procession begin! Let us offer, in Francis' name, our homage to God's creatures!"

Dancers in shimmery scarlet and green gowns swayed and circled down the aisle. They waved golden banners to the music of trumpet and drum and flute and strewed a carpet of mint and lavender and rosemary along their path.

Then began the procession of animals. Dogs and cats of every size and color led the march;

The animals and their humans began their parade.

in the pews, other dogs and cats, squirming and twitching their tails, were held firm in their owners' arms. An organ grinder with a spider monkey came next, and then a caravan of cages carrying mice and doves, a cricket, and a raven.

A young black bear somersaulted down the aisle, followed by two white wolves, walking with the wary ease of princes visiting a foreign country. Next came three black sheep with white faces, and a chestnut horse, trotting close to her policeman.

And still they came. A lithe young woman in a white gown held aloft a coconut shell bearing five red wigglers. A silver fox sniffed and followed clouds of incense rising from the altar. A peacock displayed his tail, graceful as a beautiful woman fluttering her fan. A peregrine hawk sat haughtily on the gloved hand of his falconer, and, in a sudden flurry of feathers, a snowy owl escaped

Walking with the wary ease of princes visiting a foreign country.

A snowy owl settled atop the statue of St. Francis.

his handler, settled atop the statue of St. Francis, and went to sleep.

The procession ended with an ancient gentle circus elephant, just the right size to fit within the aisle and not harm the pews. Before he began his walk, his old eyes caught sight of Martin peering yearningly over the collection baskets. He trumpeted softly and brought his trunk down to rest beside Martin.

"Come, little brother, this is not a day for hiding. Come celebrate with the rest of us. Grab hold of my trunk; don't be afraid. I won't let you go."

Francesca whispered, "Go ahead, Martin!" The reluctant skunk stepped onto the flattened trunk and felt it tighten and curl around him as he rose high into the air.

Francesca, who was not the least bit afraid, murmured to Martin, "Isn't this the most exciting adventure you ever had?"

Martin agreed that yes, indeed, it certainly was.

The elephant, with the skunk rolled high in his trunk, made his way past the astonished congregation up to the altar.

The brown-robed friar raised his hand for silence and, miraculously, the babble ceased. "My gracious Lord," he began, "we give you thanks for the beauty of the earth and sky and sea, for the songs of birds and the loveliness of flowers, for the wonders of your animal kingdom, and for our brother, Francis, for whom all these exist to praise God.

"Francis shows us that in the light of the eye of a camel is reflected the glory of God, in the work of a ladybug is the soul of an artist."

A ladybug, watching the pageant from the center of the stained glass rose window, beamed with pride.

The elephant held Martin and Francesca high in his trunk.

He saw the skunk and the cockroach looking down on him.

"So, all you creatures of the earth, show forth God's glory now! Live without fear. Go in peace to follow the good road. I bless you and ask you to bless us!"

As the friar blessed the animals with sign and holy water, he saw the skunk and the cockroach looking down on him from the elephant's trunk. He smiled, "Even you, Brother Skunk and Sister Cockroach, whom we do not usually embrace, you too have your rightful place. God has brought you here, the least of his little ones, to the head of the table, and you have behaved as royal heirs beyond reproach."

The musicians and dancers and the animals began their recessional, with the elephant now leading them back up the aisle. Martin and Francesca were the center of all eyes. To the waves of applause, Martin bowed humbly, as he imagined his patron would do, but Francesca waved and threw kisses, for she was, after all, a roach beyond reproach.

At the great door, the elephant lowered his trunk, and Martin returned to solid ground. They thanked the elephant for giving them the best seat in the house. He blinked his wise eyes and snorted softly. "Don't mention it. It was my pleasure."

Martin and Francesca began their return journey back to the soup kitchen. They did not speak, their hearts still full of the day's happenings, which would in time become part of their families' legends.

"Martin," Francesca finally spoke, "how can we proclaim God's glory?"

Martin thought for a moment and then shrugged.

"Beats me," he said. "I can't be anything other than a skunk. I like being a skunk. It suits me. But skunks don't usually go around proclaiming anyone's glory."

They began their return journey back to the soup kitchen.

If we hurry along, we can arrive in time for supper.

"And I like being a roach." She paused. "Well," she added thoughtfully, "I'm not crazy about it, but it could be worse. I could be a flea and have to spend my life on a cat, or —"

"Excuse me for interrupting, my dear, but if we hurry along, we can arrive in time for supper. I believe they'll be having something festive for the feast day—cheese puffs, or bacon rinds, fettuccini with clam sauce, Milky Ways —"

"Oh, joy," groaned Francesca, who realized she was very hungry.

"Then shall we make haste?"

"Let's!"

And so, rejoicing, they went on their way, anticipating the adventures ahead.

Ethel Pochocki's

THE BLESSING OF THE BEASTS

was designed by Barry Moser, who also
composed, drew, and engraved the illustrations.
The typeface is Herman Zapf's Palatino, designed in
1948 and issued by the Linotype Type Foundry in Frankfurt,
Germany. The calligraphy that appears on the title page, as well
as the versal W *on the opening page of the story, are the work of*
Judythe Sieck of Santa Fe, New Mexico. The book was printed for
Paraclete Press, of Brewster, Massachusetts, by Tien Wah Press of
Singapore. The paper is Grycksbo Matte from the Grycksbo Paper Mill
of Grycksbo, Sweden. · The illustrator would like to thank his wife,
Emily Crowe, for her keen insights and always honest appraisals; Jill St.
Coeur and the costume shop of the Smith College Theatre Department for
their help in costuming the Friar; Ramona Moser-Martin for her
help with setting up the flowers for Francesca and Martin's flowery
stowaway journey to the Cathedral Church of St. John the Divine.
One note of interest: the film that Martin and Francesca are
watching on page fourteen is the first horror movie ever
made: Thomas Alva Edison's 1910 Frankenstein
(with Charles Ogle portraying Mary Shelley's
monster)—the consummate outsider.